THEY'RE ALIVE!

Even though coral is a structure, reefs are alive! Simple soft corals such as zoanthids form small colonies that grow in a creeping mat.

BIG DADDY

Another reef dweller, the seahorse, breeds in an unusual way. The male has a front pouch where the female deposits her eggs. After the babies grow for a month inside the pouch, the dad hooks his tail onto a seaweed stem and rocks back and forth to help release the babies from his pouch.

The **most ancient ecosystems in the world, coral reefs may be older than 450 million years.**

PHLEGMY FISH

The two-banded anemone fish, also known as the clown fish, lives among the poisonous tentacles of the coral reef sea anemone. By secreting mucus onto its scales, this fish makes itself immune to the anemone's venom.

RED HOT

Soft fire corals protect themselves by stinging when touched. They even sting other corals that come in contact with them!

Where in the world?

Clown fish live in the tropical eastern Indian Ocean, the South China Sea, and the Western Pacific.

Predators

Sharks aren't the only predators prowling the deep—there are also sea snakes, stingrays, barracuda, and more.

While some chase down and devour their victims, others are armed with venom, which they use to kill or paralyze. Many fish have toxic flesh. Still others set traps and lie in wait for unsuspecting prey to come near. Then they attack, and so the feast begins!

TOMORROW'S DINOSAURS?
The great white shark can be up to 40 feet long. While this meat-eater has always been rare, it is now in danger of extinction. Fewer than fifty live in the waters around Australia.

> Only a few of the world's 250 species of sharks are dangerous to humans.

WAITING IN THE WINGS
Poisonous moray eels lurk around until prey comes near enough for them to clamp on with huge hinged jaws. Morays are active mostly at night, and some are over 10 feet long!

BAD MEDICINE
Sea snakes have highly toxic venom that lets them quickly overpower resistant prey. Their poison is released through fangs at the front of their mouths. The beaked sea snake has an especially lethal bite—a dose of its venom can kill fifty-three people! Despite this threat, these creatures cause very few human fatalities.

Millions of sea snakes often cluster together. In 1932, a line of intertwined sea snakes was recorded to be 10 feet wide and 62 miles long!

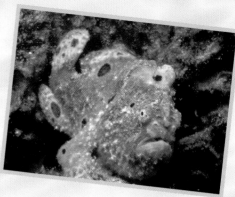

FISH BAIT

Early in life a male deep-sea angler looks for a female he can attach himself to. He plunges his needle-sharp teeth in and is fused to her. From then on, he feeds off her blood like a parasite. A female anglerfish can have up to three or four males attached to her body! When looking for prey, an anglerfish camouflages itself as a rock. Once its victim is within striking distance, the angler's huge mouth shoots forward and engulfs it. A hungry anglerfish will eat just about anything—even birds have have been found in the stomachs of dead anglers!

TOO COOL FOR SCHOOL

Barracuda have daggerlike teeth that they use to attack other fish—whole schools at a time! They have hard, bony skeletons covered by strong muscles, which help propel them swiftly through the water. These powerful muscles also allow the barracuda to accelerate in a split second.

STOP, HAMMERTIME!

The nine species of hammerhead sharks range in length from 5 to over 17 feet. Their strangely shaped heads reduce drag and act as wings that streamline these predators for fast cruising. Hammerheads have one eye on each side of their heads, which means that they can't see straight ahead of themselves. They have to swing their heads from side to side.

Where in the world?

The angler can be found from the Norwegian coast in the north to the west coast of Africa in the south. It can also be found in the Mediterranean and in the Black Sea.

LASHING OUT

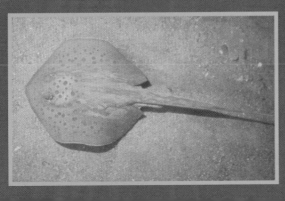

Stingrays have long tails with one or more stings, each of which has sharp spines that slash and poison their enemies.

Soft Swimmers

When you think of sea creatures, do you picture only fish with bones?

If so, think again! Octopuses, squid, jellyfish, and other members of the mollusk family are all invertebrates—which means they have no skeletons at all. And some have hardly any skin!

GETTING OUT OF DODGE

Muscular octopuses have very few stiff parts in their bodies. Attached to their pouchlike bodies are eight long arms, which they use to pull themselves along. When in need of a swift escape, they propel themselves by shooting a jet of water from their bodies. As another defense mechanism, an octopus squirts a jet of ink-colored liquid from its body to cloud its predators' vision while it makes a quick getaway.

SUPER SQUID

Believe it or not, squid are some of the most highly developed sea creatures. They can change the color of their skin almost immediately in response to environmental changes and in order to communicate simple emotions like anger or fear. Squid also have great senses. Even in the dark, they see almost perfectly. Their sense of touch is

sharp as well, for they can delicately handle fragile objects like their tiny eggs. Another incredible fact about squid is that it's actually been proved that they have a limited ability to remember things. All that is enough to make squid sound pretty cool!

When a cuttlefish is hunting, swirls of different colors and patterns flow over its skin at a dizzying rate. Cuttlefish use these skin changes to hypnotize their prey.

BE GENTLE
An octopus's skin is super-fragile—brushing by a rough object can tear its colorful surface!

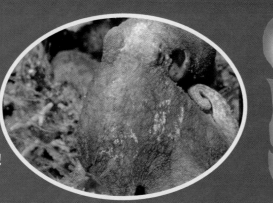

FLOATING AIMLESSLY
Some of the softest sea creatures are jellyfish, which have no skeleton and are 95 percent water. Jellyfish must rely on the ocean currents for movement because they have no real control over the direction they travel.

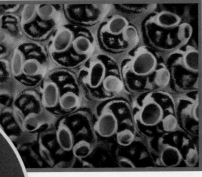

LIVING WITH THE JELLYFISH
Some fish feed on jellyfish, but others live with them for protection. Sometimes these fish learn to steer clear of the jellyfish's stinging tentacles. Other times, jellyfish get used to individual fish and don't sting them. The fish that most often live with jellyfish are young jacks and butterfish. As they get larger, they leave the protection of the jellyfish and live in large schools. The man-of-war fish spends its entire life among jellyfish.

Although no one has ever seen a living giant squid, many sea creatures bear the scars from the squid's huge suckers. The giant squid is thought to be 70 feet long and lives 2000 or more feet below the surface of the sea.

SEE-THROUGH SEA SQUIRTS
Sea squirts are almost transparent. Each sea squirt is actually a colony of individual animals connected at the base.

SOFT SLUGS
Relatives of land snails, sea slugs are made entirely of soft parts. They are usually brightly colored and under one inch long. Most sea slugs spend no time in the open water—they'd rather creep along the ocean bottom and cling to vegetation.

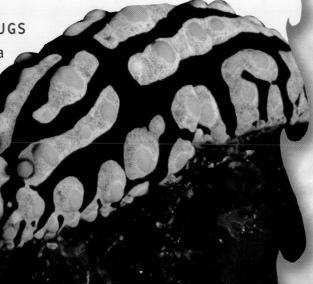

Where in the world?
The man-of-war fish can be found in warm and tropical waters in the Atlantic, Indian, and Pacific oceans.

Big Swimmers

Some of the biggest creatures in the ocean get by thanks to some of the smallest.

No matter how tasty you might look, a manta ray's bite could do very little damage. That's because it has only bottom teeth! Its mouth is just a gigantic scoop for shrimplike creatures called krill. Instead of teeth, a baleen whale has long thin plates of whalebone (called baleen) that act like a broom, sweeping through the water for food. Once the baleen has taken a big gulp of water, it filters out everything but the food. The leftover water is spit out, sometimes up to 70 tons of it! Although a whale shark does have some small teeth, it eats only krill, plankton, and tiny fish.

BIG BLUE
The blue whale is the largest mammal of all time. A record-breaking female blue whale weighing 209 tons and measuring 90 feet 6 inches was caught in 1947. That's almost as heavy as thirty elephants!

Orcas like the tongues of baleen whales, which they often take from whale carcasses.

ZOMBIE SHARK?
The whale shark, which can grow to be 45 feet, closes its eyes by retracting and rotating its eyeballs backward in the sockets.

STRUGGLING TO SURVIVE
Manatees are peaceful mammals that grow to be 14 feet long. They graze on sea grass—about 33 pounds worth each day—in warm coastal waters. One of the many threats to their survival is the motorboat; they are often killed by propellers, and numerous survivors carry scars.

Carefully pull out these sticker pages from the book.

For best glow results, expose the stickers to light and view in total darkness.

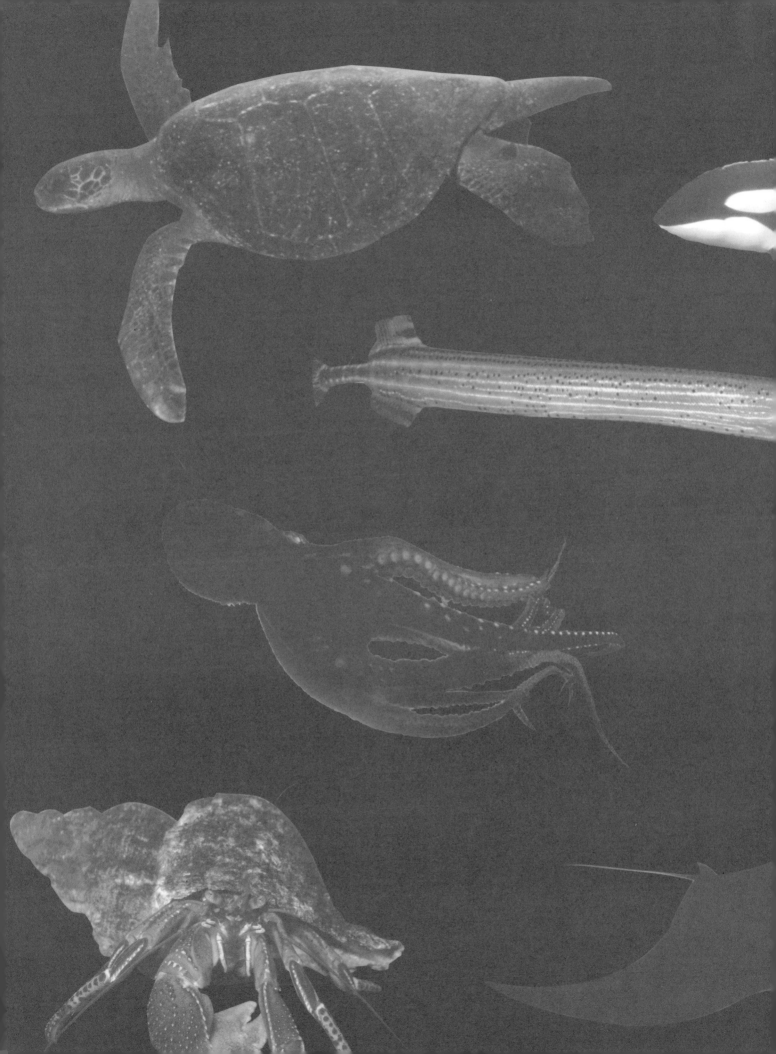

RIDING THE WAVES

The Atlantic blue marlin measures over 12 feet 4 inches. Zoologists have learned from tagging these fish that they migrate across the Atlantic Ocean.

SPECIAL SONGS

Humpback whales have unusual flippers that are scalloped along one edge. They communicate with each other by singing long, complex songs.

Whales use sonar—sound waves in water—to speak to one another across miles of ocean as well as to find prey.

NOT-SO-LEAN, MEAN KILLING MACHINE

Orcas, or killer whales, don't attack just anything that they run into. Instead, they focus on whichever creatures are common to their environment. For example, orcas living alone hunt smaller prey, while packs of orcas attack large, or multiple prey, such as other whales, sea lions, or schools of fish. This 13,000-pound predator is the only whale to hunt other warm-blooded animals.

Where in the world?

Orcas live in all of the world's oceans. Its northern and southern ranges are limited only by solid ice.

WIDE LOAD

A manta ray has large flaps that guide food to its slotlike mouth. Like sharks, the ray's skeleton is made from cartilage, not bone, which makes it very flexible. These cruising creatures can measure up to 20 feet across.

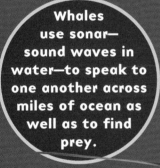

Ancient Creatures

Some of today's sea creatures look just like their ancestors did millions of years ago. While other species have evolved quite a bit, these have changed very little over the course of time.

Scientists know this from looking at fossils, remnants of living creatures that have been preserved in the earth's crust. Corals, sea urchins, and sponges, for example, could be more than twice as old as any land life. Sharks, too, are some of the oldest backboned animals in the sea and have been around for about 400 million years.

SINK OR SWIM
The chambered nautilus is a descendant of ammonites, creatures which have been extinct for 100 million years. This sea creature lives in a protective shell that has up to thirty chambers. The nautilus can change the amount of gas in each chamber to make itself float or sink in the water.

Fossilized shark teeth are common because, like today's sharks, ancient sharks lost teeth readily.

PENCIL POINT
A sea urchin, like this slate-pencil urchin, has a small mouth at the bottom of its body where it takes food in. At the top is a hole where digested food is expelled. It also has long, sharp, and sometimes poisonous spines for defense. Not many predators can argue with that!

FINE FEATHERS

A feather star has as many as 200 wispy arms and uses its tube feet to filter food from the water.

STICKING AROUND

Close relatives of sea urchins and starfish, sea cucumbers have long spiny bodies and move around on thousands of tiny tube feet. To obtain pieces of food, sea cucumbers secrete a sticky substance from their feet. They then bring the tube feet to their mouths and suck the pieces of food off. While they may not look fierce, sea cucumbers have a special way of defending themselves. When threatened, they literally push their sticky intestines out of their bodies and shoot them at their attackers.

SPARE TEETH

The lemon shark gets its name because its skin has a yellowish tint. Lemon sharks have long, thin, sharp teeth designed to spear the slippery fish that make up their meals. A young lemon shark loses an entire set of teeth every week. As teeth are lost, new ones rotate in to replace them.

COMB YOUR HAIR!

The comb jelly moves by beating together the tiny hairs that are arranged in lines down its body. Its sticky tentacles grab any small animal within reach.

Millions of years ago, cephalopods (*SEF-eh-leh-pods*) such as squid and octopuses had hard outer shells. Today the octopus has no hint of a hard shell, while some species of squid have a trace of one.

Where in the world?

The lemon shark is found in the Pacific Ocean off Central and South America, in the Atlantic Ocean off the coasts of North and South America and west Africa, in the Caribbean Sea, and in the Gulf of Mexico.

Ocean Oddballs

Some ocean dwellers can look pretty strange. They aren't expressing their individuality; they're just trying to survive!

Many sea creatures have evolved unique equipment that helps them catch prey and defend themselves from predators. Camouflage, built-in swords, lures, and poison are just a few ways some creatures protect themselves and prey on others. Others display prominent characteristics like flashy colors or spines and spikes to remind hungry predators not to mess with them. There is always a good reason for what might look weird to us humans!

SPINES AND STRIPES

The exotic lionfish shows off its venomous spines and colorful stripes to warn predators to stay away. During the day these fish stay among rocks, but at sundown they leave their hiding places to hunt for favorite meals like small fish, shrimp, and crabs. A lionfish's mouth is so large that it can swallow animals nearly the size of its own body.

PLAYING DRESS-UP

The loose, leaflike pieces of skin hanging from the leafy sea dragon's body confuse predators into thinking this sea horse is just another piece of seaweed.

SOAKING IT UP

Sponges come in all kinds of shapes—from spikes to disks to just plain blobs. Some can grow to be 6 feet high—taller than a lot of people. Sponges are made up of cells held together by needlelike spines. The spines not only support the sponge but also scare off predators. Many sponges defend themselves with harmful chemicals in their outer tissue. Scientists are experimenting to see if some of these chemicals can be used as medicines or pesticides.

JAWBREAKER

The boxfish uses its zippy yellow exterior to stave off hungry fish. Its skin is covered with poison, and underneath is a "box" of tooth-breaking bone!

PRICKLY AND PUFFY

Most of the time a porcupine fish looks as scary as a guppy. However, if threatened, it can puff itself up with either water or air into a spiky balloon that's five times its normal size. This would make it pretty hard for a predator to swallow, not to mention the poisonous, sharp spines that would give it a nasty stomachache!

NO DOUBT ABOUT IT

Early scientists disagreed about whether sponges were plants or animals. Now there's plenty of proof that sponges are animals. First, they have no chlorophyll, the chemical that plants use to make food out of sunlight. Second, they reproduce the way animals do. Sponges send sperm out through the water to fertilize eggs on the body walls of other sponges. New sponges can also be created without sexual reproduction. If you chop a living sponge into pieces and attach them to the sea bottom, each one will develop into a new sponge in less than a year.

ROCK-CLIMBING FISH

The frogfish is covered with small pieces of loose flesh that look like algae. Like its cousin the anglerfish, the frogfish uses a long strand of flesh to lure its prey. It blends easily into its surroundings while waiting motionless for its next meal to come near. Frogfish are not the swiftest of swimmers. They move by dragging themselves along the ocean floor with their fins. Some even use their fins to climb up rocks!

Where in the world?

Sponges are abundant throughout the world, especially in tropical waters like the Caribbean Sea and the Coral Sea.

Hard Shells

Life in the ocean can be dangerous—especially if you're small, soft, and tasty.

Many soft sea creatures create their own hard shells that protect them like armor against predators. The shells of crustaceans such as shrimp, crabs, and lobsters double as skeletons. The shells of mollusks like cowries and clams also keep these creatures from drying out.

A LITTLE CRABBY
Most crabs have strong protective shells and five pairs of legs. The larger of the two front pair sports strong pincers that the crab uses to crack open the shells of prey.

LIGHTWEIGHTS
Shrimp have much lighter shells than crabs or lobsters.

Red-lined shrimp work overtime as cleaners—they eat parasites and diseased tissue from larger fish such as moray eels. At times, they may even crawl fearlessly into a moray's mouth!

MEGA-MOOCHER
Unlike other crabs, the hermit crab does not create a hard shell of its own. It lives in empty shells that once belonged to other sea creatures. This is one of the potential harms of collecting shells—you might be taking away someone's future home!

ON THE MOVE
Lobsters move by swimming slowly or walking on their eight legs. Many lobsters are long-distance travelers. When winter storms hit, tens of thousands will form lines and march for up to ten miles a day along the seafloor for two or three days, until reaching deeper water.

FLAP-HAPPY
A scallop uses its shell as more than just a hiding place. It flaps the two halves back and forth in order to swim.

The only crustaceans that live on land are pill bugs and sow bugs.

SOFT AND CUTTLE-Y
Cuttlefish have a spongy shell inside their bodies called a cuttlebone. These internal shells are often hung in birdcages because they provide a soft, convenient surface for birds to rub their beaks.

TURTLES AT RISK
Sea turtles also have hard carapaces, or shells. The world's rarest turtle, the Kemp's ridley sea turtle has a gray round or heart-shaped carapace. For years, people have hunted these sea turtles for their tender meat and beautiful shells; now it is one of the most critically endangered species on earth. The Kemp's ridley turtle and other sea turtles often die because they get tangled up in fishing nets.

Where in the world?
Kemp's ridley turtles breed only in the Gulf of Mexico.

Tropical Sea Life

The warm waters around coral reefs in the tropics are home to the greatest variety of sea life on the planet.

Although there may be more life by weight in cold seas, these sea animals can't beat the vivid colors and diversity of reef-dwelling creatures.

BIG GULP
The tricky puffer lurks in red whip coral. This poisonous fish can also swell up like a water balloon, making it difficult for predators to swallow.

SNEAKY LITTLE SUCKERS
Suckers beneath the arms of a starfish help it pry open tasty shellfish.

PERFECTLY ADAPTED
Reefs feed many species of butterfly fish, whose narrow shape allows them to hide in cracks in the coral. The butterfly fish's beaklike snout and flat body also make it well suited to life weaving in and out of the crevices in a coral reef. Its tapered mouth enables it to pluck food from narrow spaces.

Reefs in Danger

Coral reefs draw visitors from all over the world. But because coral reefs are very fragile, pollution and overfishing are causing them to break down. Many tropical countries have created marine parks to protect the reefs from harmful direct contact with humans, but environmentalists still have a tough fight ahead.